For my children,

Reginald, Dominique, Tiffany, Noble, Andreu,
Quesette, Jordan, Jonathan, Mia Faye and the village,

you must know where you came from
in order to know where you are going.

Loving you always,

Ya Ya

DOMINIQUE AND THE MIRROR
Book 4: **The Reading**

© Cassie, 2018

ISBN-13: 978-0-692-11124-6 (Cassie's Stories)
ISBN-10: 0692111247

Printed in the United States of America

DOMINIQUE
and the
MIRROR

Book 4

The Reading

By

— Cassie —

Illustrations by
Amakubukuro Brown

HI, it's me again, Dominique, and it's Christmas Day. My family and I woke up early and gathered in the living room to open our presents. It was a wonderful day. Someone rang the door bell. It was a man that told my mom he had no food for his family and needed help. My mom gave him food and a gift for his little daughter so she would have a christmas too. We then got ready for church as we always do on Christmas morning. This morning my mirror was doing something different. It flashed a bright yellow light for a few seconds and then I could hear everything that was going on. I looked at my mother thinking she could hear what I was hearing, but she just looked at me and smiled. It appeared to me that no one could see this happening but me.

AS I WAS getting dressed for church the mirror showed me Adedayo in the second land, Jamaica West Indies as it was foretold by the Elders of his village. I watched as the slaves were lead off the ship. There was a overseer on horse back cracking a whip on to the backs of the slaves. I saw through the mirror how Adedayo became a very different person in this place. The mirror was showing me he could no longer hide his inner strengths. I was very worried about him. I saw that he was forced to cut down sugar cane before sun rise in the morning and was allowed to stop when it became dark. I saw Adedayo cut sugar cane day in and day out in very hot temperatures. It was unbearable. The days were long. The mirror showed my reflection and I left with my mom and dad for church.

AFTER WE RETURNED from church I went into my room to put my gifts away. I glanced at the mirror and it showed that it was night and Adedayo started going into the seeing. I could see and hear what he was hearing. He was taken back to a time of his ancestor again, Hannibal the Carthaginian as I heard him called by one of his soldiers. I read in a book my dad gave me that he was one of the greatest generals in our worlds history. I could hear a man's voice instructing his solders on what to do to prepare for a war. I could now hear what Adedayo was experiencing when he went into the seeing now. WoW! Looking in the mirror, Adedayo noticed a man who spoke the language of his home in Nigeria. He introduced himself and they became friends. He told his friend that he was going to gain his freedom at any cost. He said he had nothing left to loose. He also told his friend that his family had been taken away from him twice. First his mother and father along with his home land and the second time his wife and children, it is to much to bear.

THE MIRROR was showing me how Adedayo started strategizing as though he was playing the game of chess. There were so many people around him that felt the same as he did, including me. The slaves looked to him as their Chief. While in the fields chopping down sugar cane many of the slaves were given tasks by Adedayo. He separated them into groups with specific jobs. One group was made up of people who were strong and would be in the front of their fight for freedom, next there would be someone who could draw a map of the country and its mountains, and the most important someone to take the journals that held information on each slave that was purchased. He also found black smith's who could make weapons, a healer who could heal the injured and sick with herbs of the land and those who would forage for food, and many other jobs. They found and enlisted everyone they would need for their freedom. All of the slaves on the plantation were ready. They were waiting for Adedayo to choose the day they would be free.

MY MOM called me when all of this was happening to start family night. That is when we have pizza and ice cream that my mom makes and play games like monopoly, Jinga, and others. It is so much fun. Everything in the mirror stopped and became a mirror again. It seemed as though my mom knew I need to take a break from the mirror, but how could she? She could not see or hear what was going on or did she? We played until it was time to go to bed. And I did, I went right to sleep.

THE NEXT MORNING I heard a person saying: "No, please", over and over again, coming from the mirror. I stood in the door way of my bedroom and saw in the mirror that a slave was caught reading a book. I said, "Oh no"! I knew that slave was in trouble. All of the slaves had stopped working and turned into the direction where they heard the cry of someone pleading for their life.

AS I STOOD in the door looking in my mirror, it showed me that overseer who caught the slave reading was going to make an example of him so no other slave would want to learn how to read for fear of losing their life. My mom called everyone to breakfast. As we were sitting at the table eating, I asked the question why would someone not want a person to learn how to read or write? My father told me that it is a form of controlling a person or a people. He said knowledge is power. It allows you to think creatively, reason, question, solve problems, create and many other things that help to give you a life worth living. A educated person would recognize their poor state of living and rise up and change their circumstance by removing the person or persons controlling them. This made me think about what the mirror was showing me about Adedayo.

AFTER BREAKFAST I went back to my room waiting for the mirror to show me what happen to the slave caught reading. After a while the mirror flashed a yellow light again and I could see and hear what was going on. I saw Adedayo saying, "no more, no more"! "It is the time!" The word that Adedayo used as the war cry was "OMINIRA" (Oh-mee-nee-rah) . I used my phone to see what that word meant. The translator indicated that it is the word for freedom in the language of Yoruba in Nigeria. A slave yelled, "it has begun". I watched in the mirror as Adedayo and the slaves fought for their freedom from the inhuman way they have been treated for so many years.

THERE WAS CHAOS everywhere. Overseers were pulled off their horses, their whips and guns were snatched out of their hands. The slave that was going to be killed for reading a book fought the overseer and saved his life. I continued to watch and the mirror showed the plantation was taken over by the slaves. Adedayo was given the map that was created of the landscape and mountains by the map maker. He gave the order to gather everything thing they had planned to take and they all headed to the mountains.

THE MIRROR showed how they built a fortress in the mountains that kept overseers and authorities away. They fought so gallantly that the authorities and the governor of Jamaica realized that they could not recapture them. The authorities did not want this to happen again on the island so the governor offered Adedayo and the slaves a ship that would take them to a country where they would be free. In this country they could farm to feed themselves, and where no one would bother them.

The place was called Nova Scotia and it was located in Canada. There they where told they would live in peace and be free. They accepted the offer of the governor to take the voyage to a land where they would be free.

THE DAY CAME as the mirror showed the slaves who were now free men, women and children boarded the ship headed up the North Atlantic Ocean to Nova Scotia in Canada. Everyone participated in the duties of the daily operations of the ship. Adedayo stayed close to the captain, paying close attention to everything he did to make certain they were going to Canada . The climate suddenly changed from hot to cold when they were about half of the way to Canada going up the North Atlantic Ocean to Nova Scotia. It became very cold, just as it was where I lived in the winter in New York City. I remembered my parents had a book in our library called an atlas. It was a map of the world. I asked my dad to show me in the book where Jamaica West Indies was on the map and then Canada. I then asked my dad what was on top of Canada and he explained that Canada was close to the very top of the earth which had a climate that was extremely cold.

I WENT BACK to my room and saw in the mirror that the free slaves on the ship were experiencing the cold climate my dad just told me about. In the mirror it showed me how they were not use to the cold but they were adjusting and made warm clothing out of anything they found on the ship, they were free. They finally reached their destination. It was cold, but they were free. Everyone from the ship was welcomed by other free slaves and given food and places to stay. This made me very happy. I was looking at Adedayo through the mirror and saw that he took a deep breath and let out a loud cry as he put his feet on land. Adedayo shouted in his country's language "OMINIRA" (Oh-mee-nee-rah), which now I know means freedom, then he said in English, "I am now free!"

For now...